2024

To: My Beautiful Unicorn Princess
Kayla

From: Memom, who loves her so much.
Keep Reading !!

Purple Peaks

Rainbow River

Mermaid Cove

The Unicorn Princess

by Alyssa Schermel   Illustrated by Marina Saumell

Please write a review . . .

If you enjoy The Unicorn Princess, please take a moment to write a short review online. It will help other parents and children discover the story.

Thank you!

ISBN 978-1-7772727-1-5 (paperback)
ISBN 978-1-7772727-0-8 (hardcover)
ISBN 978-1-7772727-2-2 (deluxe edition)

www.theunicornprincess.ca

To Victoria, my partner in all things silly and ridiculous.
I couldn't have done this without you. And for Miquaes,
Paige, Dylan, Luke, Lily and Addy. xo
~A.S.

To my husband, Gustavo, and my children Luz and Agustín.
Thank you for your patience and support.
~M.S.

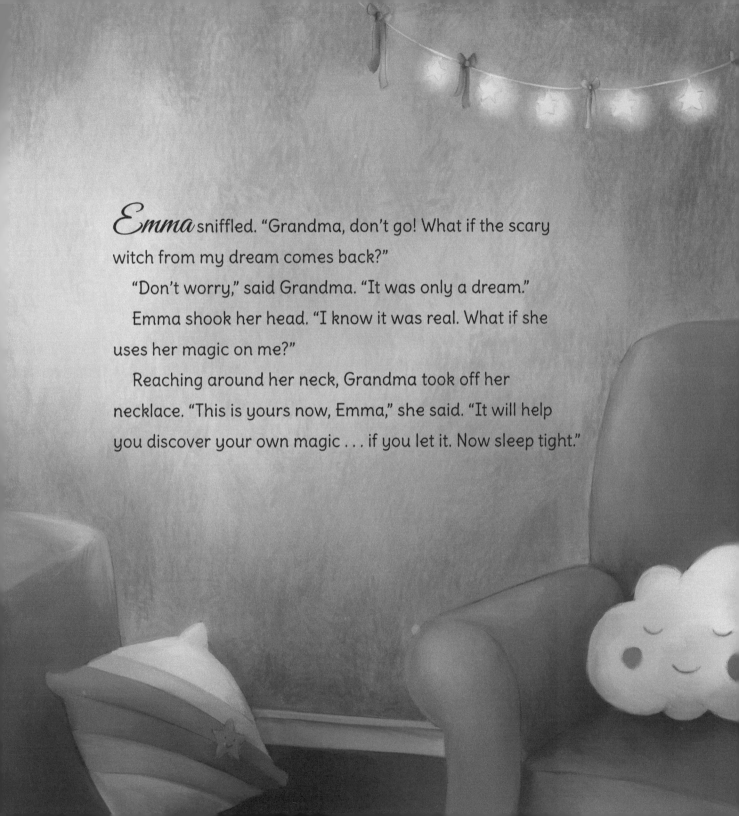

Emma sniffled. "Grandma, don't go! What if the scary witch from my dream comes back?"

"Don't worry," said Grandma. "It was only a dream."

Emma shook her head. "I know it was real. What if she uses her magic on me?"

Reaching around her neck, Grandma took off her necklace. "This is yours now, Emma," she said. "It will help you discover your own magic . . . if you let it. Now sleep tight."

But Emma couldn't sleep tight. She tossed and she turned. What did Grandma mean? *I don't have magic,* she thought. *Witches have magic. And unicorns. Unicorns have the best magic.* With that thought in mind, Emma drifted off to sleep.

"Wake up! Wake up!" a voice called.
Emma rubbed her eyes. Standing
above her was a . . . *unicorn?*
"HELP!" shouted the unicorn.
"Unicorn Valley is in terrible danger!"

"What?" Emma asked, confused.

"The witches have captured Queen Asteria and now they're turning us into pigs!" cried the unicorn. "Long ago, Queen Asteria made an enchanted barrier to keep the witches away, but they've broken it! *Please!* Come with me!"

"Come where?" Emma asked, her voice small and squeaky.

"Witch Tower," said the unicorn. "I think I can find the queen, but I need your help! I'm Flash, by the way. I'm the last unicorn left in the valley."

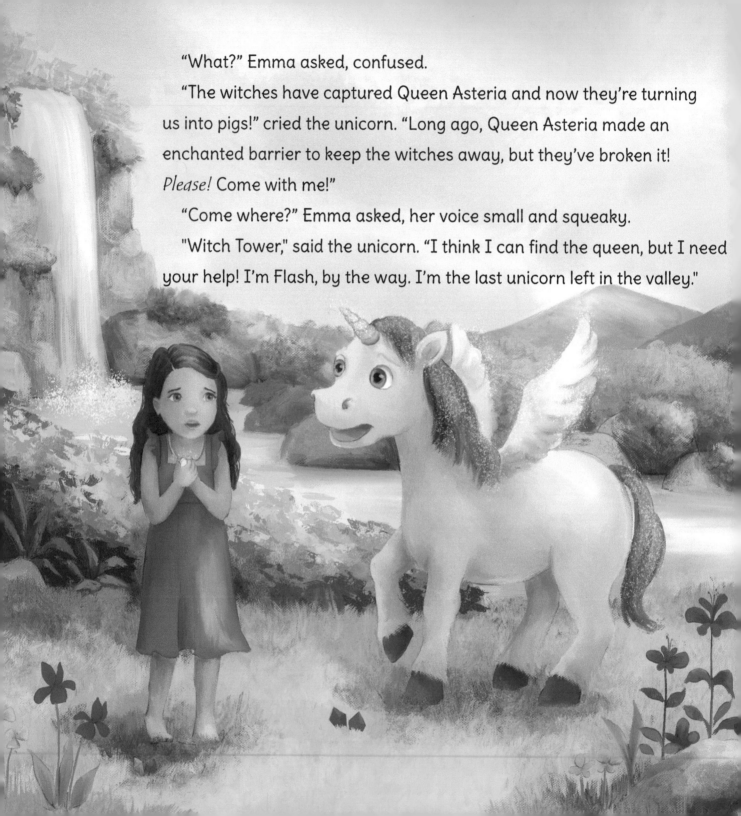

"But I don't know how to help!" Emma said, looking down at her feet. "I can't do it. I'm sorry."

"Please," said Flash. "I can't do it alone."

Emma squeezed her necklace tight. What if Grandma was right about her having magic? She took a deep breath. "I'll try . . ."

Flash fluttered his wings. "Hop on!"

As they flew higher and higher, Emma took in the land below. She had never seen anything so amazing! But even the beautiful rainbow river wasn't enough to calm her nerves. She didn't know if she had magic, but she was *sure* those evil witches did!

At last, Flash reached a spot that made Emma shudder.
"I don't like this place one bit," she said.

WITCH
TOWER

"I don't either," Flash admitted. "But we have to
go in. Grab my horn. It will make you invisible."
Trembling, Emma reached for Flash's horn.
Together, the two tiptoed toward the tower.

They searched the tower high and low, but there was no sign of Queen Asteria.

Emma knew they were running out of time.

Eternal Life Potion

* Dash of fairy dust
* Tooth of dragon
* Hair of black cat
* Breath of troll king
* Horn of unicorn queen

"We have to split up," Emma said. "You keep searching here. I'll peek in the next room."

"I don't know if that's a good idea," said Flash. "You won't be invisible if you let go of me."

Emma clutched her necklace. She had to be brave. "I promise, I'll be right back."

Emma had not taken more than three steps before a cackling filled the room.

"Look, Hexel, a visitor!" croaked the short witch. "Dropped in for a bite, did we?"

"Why yes, Grunella. I spy supper!" hissed the tall witch.

Emma shook from head to toe. Where had they come from? She had to do something—quick!

Emma grabbed a potion and threw it at Grunella's feet. It didn't help.
She threw another potion at Hexel, and another. They didn't help, either.
Nothing was working!

Psst! Over here!

Emma backed up as the witches crept toward her.
She had tried to be brave but all she'd gotten for it
was a mess and two very hungry witches.

Her eyes darted around, looking for somewhere—
anywhere—to hide.

Suddenly, she heard a whisper.

Was it Queen Asteria?

Emma leapt for the door, but there was no way around the witches.

Cackling, the two pointed their crooked fingers at Emma. Emma closed her eyes tight, waiting for the worst to happen.
ZAAAAP!

Emma opened one eye. A pig stood between her and the witches.

Flash! Emma thought. *He must have jumped in front of me!*

The witches stared, confused.

What did you do wrong?
Troll brain!
YOU did it wrong!
Pretty, pretty PRINCESS!

This has got to be the silliest argument I've ever heard! Emma thought. As she looked from one ridiculous witch to the other, her necklace began to grow warm against her heart. Something magical was happening . . .

Clasping the necklace, Emma took a big step forward. "You can turn me into a pig. Or anything you want. But you're just bad witches, and you can't scare me!"

A double rainbow flew from the necklace, scooping up the witches and carrying them away.

With the witches gone, their evil magic lifted from the land.

"Emma!" Flash exclaimed, transforming into his old self. "You did it!"

"I found my magic!" Emma said as she danced around the room. Then she remembered . . . Queen Asteria!

Emma raced to the hidden room.

"Emma," said Queen Asteria. "You have saved us all."

Flash cheered and pranced circles around Emma.

"Let us go back to Unicorn Valley and celebrate!" said the queen. "We owe you our utmost gratitude."

As they flew once more, Emma giggled with delight. This time, she could enjoy the land below.

Emma dipped her hand into the rainbow river, and her hair turned every shade of the rainbow.

"You look like one of us now," Flash said.

Later that day, the unicorns gathered.

"Emma," said Queen Asteria, "your actions at Witch Tower proved that you are no ordinary girl. Your spirit is one with ours. For your bravery, I rename you Gemma, Princess of the Unicorns."

The unicorns cheered.

"This has all been amazing!" Emma said. "I wish I could stay, but my grandma must be worried."

"Just wish on the rainbow, and you will return home," said the queen.

"I'll see you again soon, I promise!" said Emma to her new friends.
And she knew that was true. It would not be long before they would
share another magical adventure.

Purple Peaks

Rainbow River

Mermaid Cove

Unicorn Valley

Fairy Forest

Printed in the USA
CPSIA information can be obtained
at www.ICGtesting.com
LVHW062329060124
768131LV00019B/544